The Night the Chimneys Fell

by MARTY RHODES FIGLEY

Illustrated by FELICIA MARSHALL

On My Own

HISTORY

M Millbrook Press/Minneapolis

For Mary Rhodes Russell,
a Missouri mover and shaker —M.R.F.

To Paul and Kay, two special people who
always embraced my differences —F.M.

The author wishes to thank the New Madrid Historical Museum for providing information about the town and the French settlers who lived there during the 1811–1812 earthquakes.

Millbrook Press
A division of Lerner Publishing Group, Inc.
241 First Avenue North
Minneapolis, MN 55401 U.S.A.

Website address: www.lernerbooks.com

Library of Congress Cataloging-in-Publication Data

Figley, Marty Rhodes, 1948–
    The night the chimneys fell / by Marty Rhodes Figley ; illustrations by Felicia Marshall.
        p.   cm. — (On my own history)
    Summary: In 1811, nine-year-old Marie is sad to learn that her family will be moving from New Madrid, Missouri, to Saint Louis, Missouri, but when terrible earthquakes destroy her town, everything changes. Includes facts about the earthquakes and their effects.
    Includes bibliographical references.
    ISBN: 978–0–8225–7894–9 (lib. bdg. : alk. paper)
    1. New Madrid Earthquakes, 1811–1812—Juvenile fiction. [1. New Madrid Earthquakes, 1811–1812—Fiction. 2. Earthquakes—Missouri—New Madrid—Fiction. 3. Family life—Missouri—Fiction. 4. Moving, Household—Fiction. 5. New Madrid (Mo.)—History—19th century—Fiction.] I. Marshall, Felicia, ill. II. Title.
PZ7.F487Nig 2009
[E]—dc22   2008001629

Manufactured in the United States of America
1 2 3 4 5 6 – DP – 14 13 12 11 10 09

Author's Note

This story takes place in the town of New Madrid (MAD-rihd). It is located on the Mississippi River in the boot heel region of southeast Missouri. New Madrid was founded in 1789. It was originally owned by Spain. For many years, the town was an important center for trading along the river. But by 1811, only about 400 people still lived in New Madrid.

The family in this story is not real. But French people like them lived in New Madrid. Many made their living by hunting, trapping, and trading with Native Americans. On Sunday nights, after church services, the French settlers liked to have parties and dance. They danced and laughed on Sunday night, December 15, 1811. They did not know that disaster was about to strike.

She was the prettiest doll Marie
had ever seen.
Her eyes were the color of violets.
She was dressed in yellow silk and lace.
"A present for a nine-year-old young lady,"
said Uncle Charles.

Marie tried to smile.

Uncle Charles was her favorite uncle.

But she wished he weren't here right now.

He lived in Saint Louis.

It was 250 miles north of Marie's home,

New Madrid.

Both were towns along the Mississippi River.

Uncle Charles had traveled down the river on a flatboat loaded with furs.

He sold the furs in New Orleans.

Then he traveled up to New Madrid on a road called the King's Highway.

He rode a beautiful white mare he bought in New Orleans.

He named her Snow.

Uncle Charles wanted Marie's family to move to Saint Louis.

He wanted Papa to run a store with him.

Marie didn't want to go.

New Madrid had always been her home.

Saint Louis,
Missouri

New Madrid,
Missouri

MISSISSIPPI RIVER

KING'S HIGHWAY

New Orleans,
Louisiana

Uncle Charles turned to Marie's
little sister, Rose.
Marie could tell that Rose was pouting.
"Did you think I forgot you?" he asked.
He pulled another bundle from
his saddlebag.
"A five-year-old young lady needs a
New Orleans doll too."
Rose clapped her hands.
"She's dressed in pink, my favorite color!"
Mama called from the kitchen,
"Dinner is ready!"
Rose smiled at Uncle Charles.
"Mama made fancy stew and apple tart
for you," she said.

After dinner, Papa said,
"Girls, your Mama and I have made
a decision.
Business is slow in New Madrid.
This spring, we all will move to Saint Louis."

Mama touched Marie's hand.

"I know you will miss it here.

But you will have lots of cousins to play with in Saint Louis."

Marie pushed her chair away from the table.

She mumbled, "May I be excused?"

She didn't wait for an answer.

Marie ran out the front door.

She ran until she was high on the bluff
above the Mississippi.
The muddy river stretched as far
as she could see.
Big boxy flatboats floated down the river.
Strong men with poles guided narrow
keelboats up the river.
The town's white wooden houses
glowed in the late afternoon light.

Marie looked up.
The sky had filled
with hundreds of birds.
The huge black cloud of flapping wings
moved across the sky.
It seemed as if the birds were trying to
escape from something.
Marie wished her troubles could
fly away with them.

Sunday evening
December 15, 1811

"Time for bed," Marie told Rose.
Mama, Papa, and Uncle Charles had gone to
the weekly dance.
She and Rose climbed the ladder to their
bed in the loft.
Rose snuggled under the quilt.

"Don't be sad about moving," Rose said.

She hugged her doll.

"At least, we can take these," Rose said.

Marie laid her doll beside her pillow.

She curled up next to Rose.

Soon, her little sister was asleep.

Marie's eyes didn't want to shut.

She decided to walk outside to the stable.

Papa always said that Marie was good with animals.

They seemed restless tonight.

The ears on Papa's mules twitched as they watched Snow.

The mare was tossing her head and kicking her stall.

Marie stroked Snow's neck.

She whispered, "Easy, girl."

Marie stayed until the stable was quiet.

Then she went back to bed.

Later that night, she heard her parents
and Uncle Charles return.
They sounded happy.
They were laughing.
Marie's eyes filled with tears.

She looked out the window.

Sparkling stars decorated the night.

Last September, a huge, double-tailed comet had shone in the sky.

Some people said comets brought bad luck.

Maybe the comet was why they were moving.

Monday morning, 2 A.M.
December 16, 1811

Marie dreamed she was a bird.
Flying . . . no, falling, falling, falling.
But it wasn't a dream.

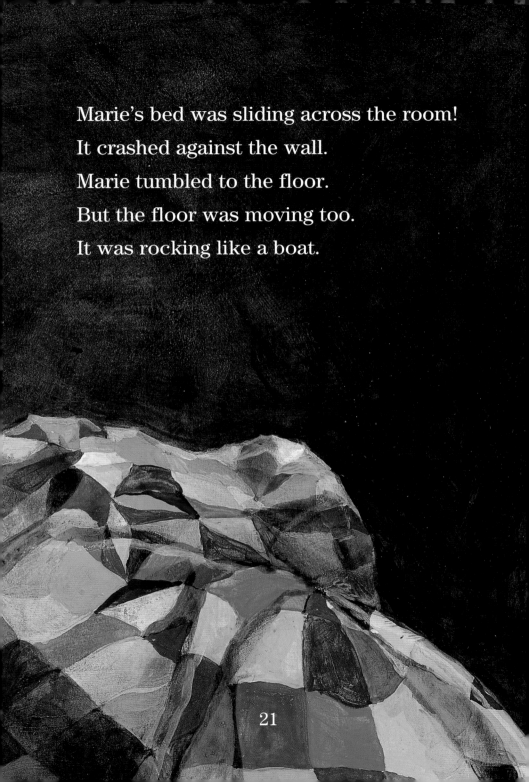

Marie's bed was sliding across the room!
It crashed against the wall.
Marie tumbled to the floor.
But the floor was moving too.
It was rocking like a boat.

In the dark, she heard Rose crying.

Marie crawled toward her.

What was happening?

Mama stumbled into the room.

"Earthquake!" she yelled.

"I have Rose!

Get out of the house now!"

Downstairs, Marie could hear dishes

crashing off the kitchen shelves.

Marie tripped over her doll.

She grabbed it and followed Mama.

Outside, Marie shivered in the dark.

Nothing was right.

The cold air was red and hazy.

It smelled like rotten eggs.

Thunder rumbled.

But it came from somewhere
deep inside the earth.

The ground rolled like a stormy ocean.

Marie heard frantic people
calling to one another.
Would the earth swallow them up?
Animals in the woods howled in terror.
Ducks and geese near the river screeched
in the dark.
Tree trunks snapped and cracked.
The river roared like an angry beast.

Marie watched Papa
lead the animals out of the stable.
He tied Snow and the mules to a fallen tree.
Mama tried to comfort Rose.
Marie felt dizzy.
She started to fall.

Strong arms caught her.

A quilt was wrapped around her.

Uncle Charles said,

"I know you are afraid, Marie.

But we will stay safe."

He gave quilts from the house to Mama
and Rose.

A small sparrow landed on Marie's shoulder.

It looked as if it was asking for help.

Then it fluttered away into the night.

The ground heaved and buckled.

The crashing sound was closer now.

The chimney on their house tumbled to
the ground!

Monday morning, 7 A.M.
December 16, 1811

Marie couldn't stop shivering.
All through the night, smaller earthquakes
shook the ground.
Everywhere, frightened people
tried to stay calm.
Papa helped an elderly neighbor
put up a tent.

The morning sun rose over broken trees.
Most of the chimneys in New Madrid
had fallen.
Several houses were burning.
Marie hugged her doll.
She hoped the awful earthquakes were over.

Rose woke up.

She started to cry.

"Marie has her new doll.

I want my doll too!" she said.

Mama pointed to their house.

"It's not safe to go inside.

The porch is leaning.

The chimney is destroyed."

Uncle Charles carried a bundle of hay
for Snow.
He put it down.
"There now, Rose," he said.
"I will fetch your doll."
"No, Charles!" said Mama.
"It's too dangerous."

Uncle Charles ignored her.

He climbed over the sagging porch.

He disappeared inside the house.

The earth started shaking again.

This time, it shook as hard as the
first earthquake.

A cow ran across the yard.

Its eyes rolled with fear.

Snow reared up.

She tried to break free of her rope.

Marie staggered over to the terrified horse.

She managed to calm Snow.

She watched as the porch
on their house collapsed.

Finally, the earth was still.

Where was Uncle Charles?

Marie looked down at the broken ground.

Her eyes blurred with tears.

She no longer cared about moving.

She wanted her uncle to be safe.

Behind her a voice said,

"The house shook all around me.

Rose's doll was hard to find!"

It was Uncle Charles.

He had a cut on his face.

His shirt was torn.

He laughed as he handed Rose her doll.

Then he hugged Marie.

"Thank you for taking care of Snow,"
he said.

"You have a gentle way with animals."

Papa and Mama took a closer look
at their house.
It was wrecked.
Many neighbors were camping
in a safer area outside of town.
Others were leaving New Madrid for good.
Marie's parents talked with Uncle Charles.
Then they walked over to Marie and Rose.

"Girls, we've decided to move
to Saint Louis now.
There is no reason to wait for spring."
Marie felt sad and relieved at the same time.
The earthquake had destroyed her home.
But Mama, Papa, Rose, and Uncle Charles
were safe.

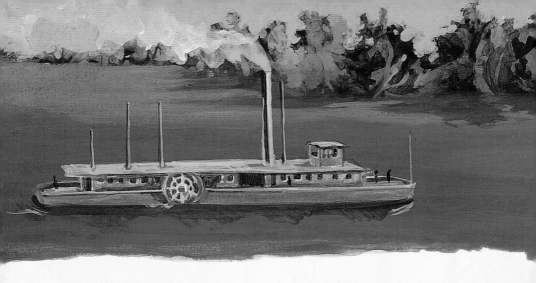

Thursday afternoon
December 19, 1811

Marie helped Papa fasten the cover
over the wagon.
It was packed with all their belongings.
Tomorrow morning they would leave
for Saint Louis.
Uncle Charles said, "Marie, come with me."
He led her to the bluff high above the river.
Down below, a crowd had gathered.
Marie gasped.

The largest boat she had ever seen was
chugging close to shore.
It was painted bright blue.
It had a huge puffing smokestack.
It wasn't like a flatboat or keelboat.
No one had to push it up the river
with poles.
A large wooden wheel on its side churned
the water.

"That's the *New Orleans*,"
said Uncle Charles.
"She's the first steamboat to travel
the Mississippi River."
He smiled at Marie.
"Steamboats can carry folks upstream
as well as down.
They make travel easier and faster.
Life on the river is changing for the better."

Marie and Uncle Charles watched
as the big boat chugged away.
They gazed down at the wrecked houses,
tumbled chimneys, and broken fences
of New Madrid.
Part of the town's shore had fallen
into the river.
Marie looked out at the wide Mississippi.

"I know you loved it here," he said.
"Just remember, the Mississippi
flows past Saint Louis too.
You'll still have your river."
Marie took Uncle Charles's hand.
"Yes," she said.
"And I'll have my family too."

Afterword

Between December 16, 1811, and February 7, 1812, some of the largest earthquakes ever recorded in the United States shook the area around New Madrid. At least three of the earthquakes—December 16, 1811, January 23, 1812, and February 7, 1812—probably measured around 8.0. Earthquakes measuring 8.0 or above cause major damage.

Strange things happened before the earthquakes. For months, a double-tailed comet shone in the sky. On September 17, the sun disappeared behind the moon, causing darkness in the middle of the day. People also reported strange animal behavior before and during the earthquake. Horses were skittish. Wild animals lost their fear of humans and other animals. Deer, wolves, and bears came out of the woods together.

Not many people lived in the area where the earthquakes occurred. Perhaps fewer than 100 people died. But no one knows how many people died on the river or how many Native Americans in the area lost their lives. Towns were destroyed, islands disappeared, and lakes formed. For a few hours, the Mississippi River ran backward.

A huge area of the country (over 1.5 million square miles) was affected. Close to 2,000 smaller earthquakes were recorded throughout the central and eastern United States. Dishes cracked in New York City. Bells rang in

Richmond, Virginia. Walls shook in Detroit, Michigan, and clocks stopped in Charleston, South Carolina.

New Madrid was almost destroyed by the largest quakes. The December 16 earthquake shook down most of the town's chimneys. A quake on February 7 destroyed the remaining houses. Many people escaped to higher ground 30 miles north of the town. They lived for almost a year in tents and shacks. The citizens of New Madrid did rebuild. By 2006, the town had a population of around 3,100.

Bibliography

Bagnall, Norma Hayes. *On Shaky Ground.* Columbia: University of Missouri Press, 1996.

Bradbury, John. *Travels in the Interior of America.* London: Sherwood, Neely, and Johnes, 1819.

Feldman, Jay. *When the Mississippi Ran Backwards.* New York: Free Press, 2005.

Flint, Timothy. *Recollections of the Last Ten Years.* Boston: Cummings, Hilliard, 1826.

Fuller, Myron L. *The New Madrid Earthquake.* 1912. Reprint, Marble Hill, MO: Gutenberg-Richter Publications, 1995.

Latrobe, J. H. B. *The First Steamboat Voyage on Western Waters.* Baltimore: John Murphy, 1871.

Logston, David R. *"I Was There!" in the New Madrid Earthquakes of 1811–12.* Nashville: Kettle Mills Press, 1990.

McCall, Edith. *Biography of a River.* New York: Walker and Company, 1990.

Penick, James Lal, Jr. *The New Madrid Earthquakes.* Rev. ed. Columbia: University of Missouri Press, 1988.